TRIANGLE HISTORIES
★ ★ ★ ★ ★ ★ ★ ★ ★
THE REVOLUTIONARY WAR

THE BATTLE OF HARLEM HEIGHTS

Mary Hertz Scarbrough

BLACKBIRCH®
PRESS

THOMSON
★
GALE

San Diego • Detroit • New York • San Francisco • Cleveland • New Haven, Conn. • Waterville, Maine • London • Munich

Photo credits: cover, pages 9, 10, 12, 20 © Bettman/CORBIS; pages 5, 7, 14, 22 © North Wind Picture Archives; pages 11, 15, 27 © Hulton/Archive, Getty Images; page 12 © New York Historical Society, New York, USA/The Bridgeman Art Library; page 16 © Mary Evans Picture Library; page 17 © Library of Congress/The Bridgeman Art Library; page 18 © Lee Snider/CORBIS; page 19 © The Bridgeman Art Library; page 21 © Dover Publications; pages 28, 29 © The Art Archive/Chateau de Bierancourt/Dagli Orti

LIBRARY OF CONGRESS CATALOGING-IN-PUBLICATION DATA

Scarbrough, Mary Hertz.
  Battle of Harlem Heights / by Mary Hertz Scarbrough.
      p. cm. — (Triangle history of the American Revolution series. Revolutionary War battles)
  Summary: Describes the people and action of Revolutionary War battles that took place in New York, particularly the Battle of Harlem Heights, which underscored General Washington's battle philosophy and boosted the morale of his troops.
  Includes bibliographical references (p.) and index.
    ISBN 1-56711-777-5 (alk. paper)
  1. Harlem Heights, Battle of, N.Y., 1776—Juvenile literature. [1. Harlem Heights, Battle of, N.Y., 1776. 2. United States—History—Revolution, 1775-1783—Campaigns.] I. Title. II. Series.

  E241.H2S28 2004
  973.3'32—dc21   2003004212

Printed in China
10 9 8 7 6 5 4 3 2 1

CONTENTS

Preface: The American Revolution

Today, more than two centuries after the final shots were fired, the American Revolution remains an inspiring story not only to Americans, but also to people around the world. For many citizens, the well-known battles that occurred between 1775 and 1781—such as Lexington, Trenton, Yorktown, and others— represent the essence of the Revolution. In truth, however, the formation of the United States involved much more than the battles of the Revolutionary War. The creation of our nation occurred over several decades, beginning in 1763, at the end of the French and Indian War, and continuing until 1790, when the last of the original thirteen colonies ratified the Constitution.

More than two hundred years later, it may be difficult to fully appreciate the courage and determination of the people who fought for, and founded, our nation. The decision to declare independence was not made easily—and it was not unanimous. Breaking away from England—the ancestral land of most colonists—was a bold and difficult move. In addition to the emotional hardship of revolt, colonists faced the greatest military and economic power in the world at the time.

The first step on the path to the Revolution was essentially a dispute over money. By 1763 England's treasury had been drained in order to pay for the French and Indian War. British lawmakers, as well as England's new ruler, King George III, felt that the colonies should help to pay for the war's expense and for the cost of housing the British troops who remained in the colonies. Thus began a series of oppressive British tax acts and other laws that angered the colonists and eventually provoked full-scale violence.

The Stamp Act of 1765 was followed by the Townshend Acts in 1767. Gradually, colonists were forced to pay taxes on dozens of everyday goods from playing cards to paint to tea. At the same time, the colonists had no say in the passage of these acts. The more colonists complained that "taxation without representation is tyranny," the more British lawmakers claimed the right to make laws for the colonists "in all cases whatsoever." Soldiers and tax collectors were sent to the colonies to enforce the new laws. In addition, the colonists were forbidden to trade with any country but England.

Each act of Parliament pushed the colonies closer to unifying in opposition to English laws. Boycotts of British goods inspired protests and violence against tax collectors. Merchants who continued to trade with the Crown risked attacks by their colonial neighbors. The rising violence soon led to riots against British troops stationed in the colonies and the organized destruction of British goods. Tossing tea into Boston Harbor was just one destructive act. That event, the Boston Tea Party, led England to pass the so-called Intolerable Acts of 1774. The port of Boston was closed, more British troops were sent to the colonies, and many more legal rights for colonists were suspended.

Finally, there was no turning back. Early on an April morning in 1775, at Lexington Green in Massachusetts, the first shots of the American Revolution were fired. Even after the first battle, the idea of a war against England seemed unimaginable to all but a few radicals. Many colonists held out hope that a compromise could be reached. Except for the Battle of Bunker Hill and some minor battles at sea, the war ceased for much of 1775. During this time, delegates to the Continental Congress struggled to reach a consensus about the next step.

During those uncertain months, the Revolution was fought, not on a military battlefield, but on the battlefield of public opinion. Ardent rebels—especially Samuel Adams and Thomas Paine—worked tirelessly to keep the spirit of revolution alive. They stoked the fires of revolt by writing letters and pamphlets, speaking at public gatherings, organizing boycotts, and devising other forms of protest. It was their brave efforts that kept others focused on liberty and freedom until July 4, 1776. On that day, Thomas Jefferson's Declaration of Independence left no doubt about the intentions of the colonies. As John Adams wrote afterward, the "revolution began in hearts and minds not on battlefield."

As unifying as Jefferson's words were, the United States did not become a nation the moment the Declaration of Independence claimed the right of all people to "life, liberty, and the pursuit of happiness." Before, during, and after the war, Americans who spoke of their "country" still generally meant whatever colony was their home. Some colonies even had their own navies during the war, and a few sent their own representatives to Europe to seek aid for their colony alone while delegates from the Continental Congress were doing the same job for the whole United

The Minuteman statue stands in Concord, Massachusetts.

States. Real national unity did not begin to take hold until the inauguration of George Washington in 1789, and did not fully bloom until the dawn of the nineteenth century.

The story of the American Revolution has been told for more than two centuries and may well be told for centuries to come. It is a tribute to the men and women who came together during this unique era that, to this day, people the world over find inspiration in the story of the Revolution. In the words of the Declaration of Independence, these great Americans risked "their lives, their fortunes, and their sacred honor" for freedom.

Introduction:
"We'll Alter Your Tune"

All through the summer of 1776, American troops watched uneasily as boatload after boatload of British soldiers sailed into the waters around Staten Island, Long Island, and New York Island (now called Manhattan). Week after week, the British arrived. By late summer, as many as thirty-two thousand British soldiers awaited the command to attack the rebellious colonists. The American forces numbered about twenty thousand.

The Americans had much more than a shortage of troops to overcome. The Continental army, led by General George Washington, was untrained, undisciplined, and often unhealthy, and never had enough supplies. The British troops were the opposite in nearly every way.

Strength at sea and on land meant that the British could fight almost anywhere, which kept the Americans guessing where the attack would happen. The Americans were completely unprepared to do battle at sea. The Continental Congress had authorized an American navy just months earlier, but so far the navy was more a dream than a reality. In contrast, officers with battle experience commanded Great Britain's navy, the world's largest. The many waterways in the region gave the British many options for coming ashore. On shore, the Americans did not have enough soldiers to defend large areas of land.

The first attack came in late August on Long Island. The British claimed a decisive victory, and American losses were high.

General George Washington directed his troops' nighttime retreat after the British victory in the Battle of Long Island.

Defeated, the Continental army retreated to New York Island.

In mid-September some of the British forces anchored near Kip's Bay, an area north of New York City on the East River, as they prepared for their next strike. When American guards, making their rounds along the shore, cried, "All is well," British sailors shouted back, "We'll alter your tune before tomorrow night."

The British came ashore at Kip's Bay on September 15. The Americans dropped their muskets, coats, and knapsacks— anything that would slow them down—and fled as a few dozen British soldiers approached. An enraged Washington ordered his men to stand and fight, but it was no use. From Kip's Bay the British marched the short distance to New York City. The Americans scrambled to evacuate the city before the enemy arrived.

The next morning, the two sides skirmished near Harlem Heights, north of Kip's Bay. This time, the Americans did not flee from the enemy. Although they fought well, they were greatly outnumbered and had begun to retreat when British buglers taunted them with a tune. The buglers played the call of foxhunters who have trapped or killed their prey and are ending the chase.

The buglers picked the wrong tune. The Americans soon rallied. That afternoon, Washington's ragtag army saw something it had never seen before: the fleeing backs of the enemy.

7

General George Washington, Commander in Chief

Great Britain's American colonies had no army, only loosely organized militias around Boston, when the Second Continental Congress in Philadelphia appointed George Washington to head a Continental army in June 1775. Congressional delegates chose Washington partly because they believed he would be a good leader and could unite northern and southern patriots into one cause. Washington was unsure. He told Congress, "I do not think myself equal to the command I am honored with." He told others that the command he had been given was "too boundless for my abilities and far, very far beyond my experience." The Continental Congress placed its trust in Washington, however, and promised to "maintain and assist and adhere" to him "with their lives and fortunes."

Washington had become famous for his courage during the French and Indian War two decades earlier. His peers considered him a man of integrity, courteous, honest, and respectful. As a military leader, he had a reputation as a good listener.

First Success

Washington first saw the enormity of the task before him when he arrived in Massachusetts in July 1775 to take control of the local militias and begin to mold them into the Continental army. Everyday challenges for the army in Massachusetts included scarce supplies, widespread illness, a lack of discipline and training, short-term enlistments, and frequent desertions. At one point, Washington discovered that each soldier only had enough gunpowder to fire about nine shots.

The British evacuated troops and Loyalists from Boston in March 1776, allowing the patriots to reclaim the city.

After the battles at Lexington and Concord in April 1775, the patriots took control of the land around Boston and trapped the British in the city. For months, neither side made a move. Finally, in early March 1776, Washington ordered some troops to move to the high ground of Dorchester Heights. Under artillery cover, the patriots built defenses upon the frozen ground and aimed their cannons at Boston. They wanted to provoke either an evacuation of the city or an attack. They were sure that their superior position would guarantee a victory over the British, who were worn out from the long winter with scarce supplies. The British prepared to attack, but when a storm delayed them, they reconsidered. On March 7 the British began to evacuate troops and Loyalists (British sympathizers) from Boston. The siege ended without an exchange of gunfire. The British boarded their ships and sailed away on March 17.

That same day, patriot troops entered Boston to reclaim the city. Washington marched in the next day, but wasted no time

9

Militia Soldiers

Many soldiers who served in the Revolutionary War were not part of the regular Continental army, but were members of militias. The first American militia formed in 1608 in the Jamestown colony in Virginia with the blessing and encouragement of England. Militias were necessary to protect colonists from rebellious slaves, the French, and hostile Native American tribes.

Militiamen were citizen soldiers. That is, they were citizens first and soldiers second, and served only when needed. Militias, it was believed, should be allied with their homes and communities. Colonists generally had a distrust of a standing (professional) army. They believed a standing army was allied only to a sovereign or king, and might be used to abuse citizens' liberties.

At the beginning of the Revolutionary War, many leaders were confident that the militiamen would be skilled in battle. The militiamen did not prove to be as capable as hoped. Untrained and undisciplined, the militiamen developed a reputation for fleeing under fire. Enlistment terms, the amount of time a militiaman was signed up to be in the army, were short—usually three months. This sometimes led to disaster. In the second Battle of Saratoga in October 1777, militiamen deserted in the middle of battle. They claimed that their enlistments were over.

Historians have estimated that between 250,000 to 375,000 militiamen served during the war. Many did not engage in combat but performed guard duties and other jobs. At Kip's Bay on September 15, 1776, more than half of the American soldiers were either militiamen or other recruits who also had short-term enlistments. Some of the men had been in service less than a week. Many who fled from the British at Kip's Bay proved their bravery later in the war.

The early Revolutionary War depended on militiamen, who were not part of a formal army.

enjoying the victory. He had already guessed that New York would be the next British target. He reasoned that New York "secures the free and only communication between the Northern and Southern colonies, which will be entirely cut off by their possessing it, and give them the command of Hudson's River and an easy pass into Canada." The Continental army arrived in New York by mid-April, and Washington put the men to work building fortifications.

The Battle of Long Island

Washington's prediction that the British would soon appear in New York proved correct. In late June the British began to arrive in the area and had soon assembled a huge force. Admiral Richard Howe commanded the British navy. His brother, General William Howe, led the army. At first the British forces stayed on and around Staten Island. On August 22, as the Americans watched, thousands of British and German soldiers landed on

Long Island. The German soldiers, often called Hessians, had been hired from German princes to add to the British ranks.

Washington suspected that the Long Island landing might be a way for the British to distract the Americans from the main attack site, so he divided his troops between Long Island and New York Island. This meant that the British, who had landed about twenty thousand troops on Long Island, outnumbered their American counterparts there by more than two to one.

Outnumbered by British troops, American soldiers on Long Island fled across the East River to New York Island.

The British Commanders: William Howe and Richard Howe

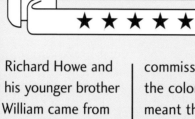

Admiral Richard Howe

General William Howe

Richard Howe and his younger brother William came from an aristocratic and military family. Their older brother, George, was a hero who died during the French and Indian War (1756–1763). William, too, gained the respect of his men for his courageous actions during that war. Richard was a compassionate leader who was respected by his men. His military skills were not strongly evident until near the end of his time in America.

Lord Richard Howe (admiral) was the commander in chief of the British naval forces in America from February 6, 1776, to September 11, 1777. Sir William Howe (general) was the commander in chief of the British army in America, from 1775 through the spring of 1778. King George III also appointed the brothers as peace commissioners to the colonies. This meant that the Howes were sent to America not only to fight with the Americans but also to try to end the war peacefully.

Admiral Howe in particular struggled with the conflict presented by his dual roles. Before the war began, he tried to resolve the conflict between England and the colonies. He continued his peace-making efforts when he arrived in America. General Howe, on the other hand, was more eager to end the war by defeating the rebellious colonists.

Both Howes were criticized in Great Britain for their slowness in conducting the war. They often delayed attacks for weeks, when it appeared to others that a swift attack would result in a victory for the British.

Washington was mistaken. The British did not attack New York Island, but concentrated all efforts on Long Island. The fiercest fighting took place on August 27. The Americans had hoped to secure Brooklyn Heights, overlooking the East River, but the British outwitted them.

During the fighting, many of the American soldiers either fled or surrendered. Some, particularly those who served under General William Alexander (also known as Lord Stirling), fought heroically, only to be nearly wiped out. American losses were significant—estimates ranged from eleven hundred to fifteen hundred, which included more than one thousand captured and the rest injured or dead. The day ended with the Americans trapped with the East River behind them, and a huge British force ready to assault from the front. For the next two and a half days, the cornered Americans awaited the next British move.

★

In August 1776 delegates in Philadelphia signed the formal parchment copy of the Declaration of Independence.

★

A Brilliant Military Maneuver in the Face of Defeat

The Continental army seemed to have no option but to wait for an attack. The hours passed as the troops battled heavy rains, exhaustion, and a lack of food. On Thursday, August 29, one soldier wrote, "The Trenches, Forts, Tents, & Camp are overflowed with water, & yet our Men must stand exposed themselves . . . . Twenty four hours at least the Lines are manned by the same Persons, & some Regiments have been on duty since Monday!"

Washington turned the hopeless situation into a challenge. At work in his nearby headquarters, he made plans known only to a few. He summoned every available boat and pretended that the boats would be used to bring in relief troops for the trapped soldiers. Instead he launched a daring retreat late on August 29, as the boats ferried his troops across the East River to New York. Heavy fog helped muffle the sound. Between nine

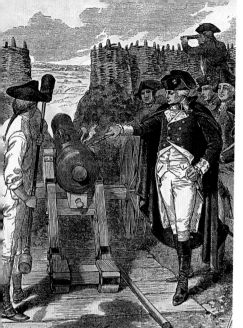

Washington was both praised and criticized for his actions on Long Island.

thousand and twelve thousand men, along with munitions and supplies, disappeared overnight from within six hundred yards of the British soldiers. In the morning, the British discovered that the Americans had vanished.

Washington later wrote to Congress that he "had hardly been off my horse and had never closed my eyes" in days. Many people viewed the near-miraculous retreat as proof of Washington's outstanding military skills. Others saw it differently and criticized him because of his attempt to defend Long Island, his division of troops between New York Island and Long Island, and because the Americans had been outwitted by the British at Brooklyn Heights.

New York: Defend, Burn, or Abandon?

Two issues bothered Washington as summer turned to fall in 1776. He worried constantly about the quantity and quality of his troops. Morale was low. Militiamen headed home in droves. Washington reported to Congress, "Great numbers of them have gone off; in some instances almost by whole regiments, by half ones, and by companies at a time. . . . Till of late, I had no doubt in my own mind of defending this place; nor should I have yet, if the men would do their duty, but this I despair of." He had good reason to be afraid. For example, within days of the Long Island battle, the number of militiamen from Connecticut dwindled from eight thousand to two thousand.

The other issue, the fate of New York City, demanded a quick decision. After the Battle of Long Island, all signs pointed to another British attack, with the enemy's ultimate goal the capture of New York. Washington needed to decide whether to try to defend the city, to evacuate it, or to take some other action. As Washington knew, the British wanted to capture the city because they understood its significance to America. It was an important gateway between the northern colonies and the southern ones.

The British also wanted to use the city for their winter headquarters. To prevent that, Washington asked Congress for permission to burn the city. On September 6, word reached Washington that Congress wanted no damage done to the city.

About twenty thousand people lived in New York City in 1776, approximately two-thirds of whom were Loyalists. The city occupied slightly less than the lower three miles of New York Island. The British could easily reach the city either by land or by water. Their superior strength made a successful American defense highly unlikely.

Washington called his top advisers to a council of war on September 7 to make a decision about New York. Washington thought that a total evacuation might be best but wanted to listen to other ideas. His advisers were split into three groups. General Israel Putnam wanted a complete and immediate evacuation. General Hugh Mercer was ill and unable to attend the meeting, but in a letter he argued for defense of the city, and General William Heath agreed. General Nathanael Greene supported evacuation and destruction of the city.

Washington called a council of war to decide the fate of New York City, an important gateway between the northern and southern colonies.

The Battle of Harlem Heights

The council decided on a compromise that would neither fully protect nor completely abandon the city. The plan was to spread American resources over the 13-mile length of New York Island, as the American leaders tried to determine where the British would launch their next attack. The American soldiers were placed at various locations that the leaders had determined were likely places for the British to launch their next attack. Putnam, along with five thousand troops, remained in the city to defend it. A limited evacuation began. Heath took nine thousand troops to the upper part of the island, near King's Bridge, to stop any enemy landing attempts. King's Bridge was important because it was the only connection between the island and the mainland. Some men were stationed at Fort Washington, south of King's Bridge. In between Putnam and Heath, five thousand troops were stationed near Turtle Bay and Kip's Bay, north of the city on the East River, where the British could come ashore. Meanwhile, throughout early September the British commanders assembled troops in different locations within striking distance of the city and in the waters and small islands surrounding New York Island.

On September 11, Nathanael Greene and others asked to reconsider the September 7 decision to defend New York City. Washington agreed because he was becoming more and more concerned about his divided army. The next day a second war

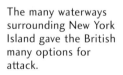

The many waterways surrounding New York Island gave the British many options for attack.

Long Island Peace Conference of September 11, 1776

In July 1776 Admiral Richard Howe and General William Howe tried to engage Washington in peace negotiations. Washington declined because he did not believe that the Howes had the power to make a binding peace agreement. When the British captured American general John Sullivan during the Battle of Long Island, Admiral Howe decided to try

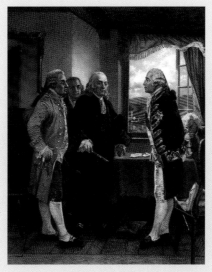

Benjamin Franklin (center) and other delegates from the Continental Congress met with General Howe to discuss peace.

again. He sent Sullivan on a mission to the Continental Congress in Philadelphia, to request a peace conference.

Congress was not sure how to respond. On the one hand, to enter talks might make it appear as though the Americans were having doubts about fighting for independence. On the other hand, it did not seem right to say no to the possibility of a peaceful settlement. In the end, Congress appointed Benjamin Franklin, John Adams, and Edward Rutledge to meet with Howe.

The meeting took place on September 11 on Staten Island. Howe confirmed the Americans' suspicions that he had no power to make a treaty with Congress. He told them that he would have to get approval from the king for any proposed agreement. Moreover, he had no authority to enter negotiations that would result in independence for the colonies. Hearing this, the Americans ended the meeting. The parties parted on good terms; Franklin and Howe were old acquaintances who had discussed the colonial situation when Franklin had been in England before the war.

Sullivan was released during a prisoner exchange later in September.

council voted to evacuate nearly all of New York Island south of the Harlem River. They made an exception for Fort Washington, where eight thousand troops were posted. The remaining troops were to be brought together in one force on the plains of Harlem.

Toward evening on September 13, a forty-gun British ship fired at the Americans on the shore of the East River. British soldiers on Governor's Island also fired at the Americans. As he investigated the situation, Washington narrowly missed being hit by a cannonball that struck six feet from him. The next evening, more British ships arrived at the islands in Hell Gate, where the East River and Long Island Sound meet, and joined other enemy soldiers already there.

The Morris-Jumel mansion served as Washington's head-quarters during the Battle of Harlem Heights.

Disaster at Kip's Bay

Without Washington's knowledge, around dawn on September 15, five British warships anchored between Kip's Bay and Turtle Bay. From these warships the British boasted to the Americans onshore, "We'll alter your tune before tomorrow night." Also around dawn, three other warships, the *Renown*, the *Pearl*, and the *Repulse*, made their way toward Bloomingdale, north of the city on the Hudson River.

Around 10 A.M. the Americans also spotted flatboats on the East River, a sign that the British intended to transport large numbers of soldiers for a landing. It seemed that the British planned to attack the island from both sides at the same time.

The quiet and uncertainty ended around eleven o'clock that morning. Fire boomed from more than eighty cannons aboard British ships near Kip's Bay. For an hour or more, the bombardment pinned the patriots to their lines—shallow ditches dug along the bank of the East River. Through the haze from the ships' cannons, the American troops returned fire as best they could. The fierce gunfire held other American troops a half mile back from the shore. Meanwhile, the intense smoke and the roaring guns allowed eighty-four boats of British and Hessian soldiers to row across the river without being seen. The British guns quieted, and then the Americans heard splashing and shouted commands. As the smoke drifted away, they caught their first glimpse of the approaching enemy. At first only sixty or seventy enemy troops advanced on the Americans.

The American troops did not open fire. Instead, they panicked and fled. They dropped anything that might slow their retreat. One soldier later wrote, "The ground was literally covered with arms [guns], knapsacks, staves, coats, hats," left by the escaping soldiers.

Washington galloped up on his horse in the middle of this chaos, just as more American troops arrived from the city. These soldiers and officers fled too as Washington tried to rally them. Enraged, he threw his hat upon the ground and exclaimed, "Are these the men with whom I am to defend America?" and "Good God, have I got troops such as these?" He tried to whip officers and soldiers as they flew by him. The men did not stop. Within minutes, twenty-five hundred soldiers had thrown down their weapons and fled.

British troops approached New York City from both the Hudson River (pictured) on the west and the East River.

The approaching British narrowly missed the chance to capture the American commander in chief. Washington's anger at his troops made him forget his own safety. He sat on his horse, frozen at the scene, and without any way to defend himself. An aide finally grabbed the bridle of Washington's horse and led him to safety. Nathanael Greene later wrote that Washington was within eighty yards of the enemy and was so "vexed he sought death rather than life."

Further south, in New York City, Israel Putnam rushed to evacuate the area before the British arrived. He headed toward Harlem Heights with a line of troops and city residents that stretched for two miles. The Heights were north of the city and bordered the Hudson River just west of Harlem, a village near the mouth of the Harlem River. The road that Putnam and the evacuees traveled, called the Bloomingdale Road, exposed them to enemy fire from the ships anchored on the Hudson. Moreover, the evacuees included many exhausted and thirsty women and children. Putnam worked tirelessly during the hot and dusty 12-mile march to ensure their safety.

Because the evacuation had to be carried out so quickly, Putnam had to abandon most of the heavy cannons (sixty-seven of them) and much of the provisions and military stores in the city. The costly and difficult march could have easily turned

After an attempt to rally his troops failed, Washington (pictured on horseback) was nearly captured by the British.

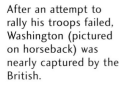

disastrous. The British missed an opportunity to stretch troops across the island from Kip's Bay to the Hudson and completely cut off the retreat.

Even so, American losses were high. Seventeen officers and 350 men were lost, mostly missing and captured. The British now controlled New York City. The loss, in terms of morale, was devastating. Nevertheless, the Americans refused to surrender the entire island without a fight.

Harlem Heights

By the evening of September 15, about nine thousand American soldiers, including those from Kip's Bay, had gathered in the Harlem Heights area. Woods and small hills helped conceal the troops. To the west of the Americans was the Hudson River; to the south and slightly east stood the plains of Harlem; and directly to the south was a small valley called Hollow Way.

Washington directed General Joseph Spencer's troops and some of Putnam's to a plateau about a mile in length on the heights. They immediately started to build defenses. Heath commanded an additional four thousand or five thousand soldiers at King's Bridge. Greene's men, the southernmost troops, overlooked Hollow Way. These troops would most likely be the first to meet the advancing enemy. The closest British, meanwhile, were camped about one and one-half miles from Greene's troops, south of the Hollow Way.

The night passed without incident. An American scouting mission went out before dawn on September 16, led by Thomas Knowlton. Knowlton commanded the Rangers, an elite group posted at the front to track the movements of the enemy. Around sunrise, at a stone house known as Jones's farmhouse, the Rangers encountered

General William Heath defended the American position at King's Bridge.

British soldiers and American Rangers clashed in the small valley of Hollow Way at the beginning of the Battle of Harlem Heights.

some British pickets, a small group of soldiers posted to guard nearby British troops from a surprise attack. The pickets spotted Knowlton's men, and some of them opened fire. A half hour skirmish followed between 120 Rangers and a few hundred British. One of the Rangers later reported that the enemy "marched up within six rods [about one hundred feet] of us, and then formed to give us battle which we were ready for; and Colonel Knowlton gave orders to fire, which we did, and stood theirs till we perceived they were getting their flanking guards around us."

The Rangers fired about eight rounds apiece. Then Knowlton ordered a retreat because the British had called for reinforcements. The outnumbered Rangers made a quick and orderly retreat toward the American front lines, while the British followed them through woods and farm fields.

Adjutant General Joseph Reed, Washington's aide, observed the Rangers and reported that they "behaved well stood & return'd the Fire till overpowered by the numbers they were obliged to retreat." Meanwhile, Washington, with Greene above Hollow Way, heard the firing between the Rangers and the British.

The troops above Hollow Way prepared for battle. When the British did not immediately advance, Putnam's and Spencer's

Lieutenant Colonel Thomas Knowlton and the Rangers

Thomas Knowlton, born in 1740, was only fifteen when he distinguished himself as a soldier during the French and Indian War. In the Battle of Bunker Hill in Massachusetts on June 17, 1775, Knowlton and his Connecticut militiamen displayed bravery and ingenuity. Against impossible odds, they managed to hold an exposed position against British attacks. Knowlton's courage and intelligence caught the attention of Washington.

After the Battle of Long Island, Knowlton put together a small corps of "Rangers"— about 120 volunteers from Connecticut and other eastern regiments—to be posted at the front to watch the enemy's movements. Knowlton's sixteen-year-old son and brother were members as well, and fought alongside him at the Battle of Harlem Heights.

Knowlton was respected by his superiors and admired by his men for his military skills, his leadership abilities, his courteous manner, and his courage. Washington called Knowlton "the gallant and brave Colonel Knowlton who would have been an honor to any Country."

The Rangers were captured with Fort Washington on November 16, 1776.

men went to work with spades and shovels to dig entrenchments. They wanted to fortify two lines that the British would have to break through if they planned to advance.

As the Rangers retreated across Hollow Way and hurried onto the Heights, British troops appeared on some high ground

23

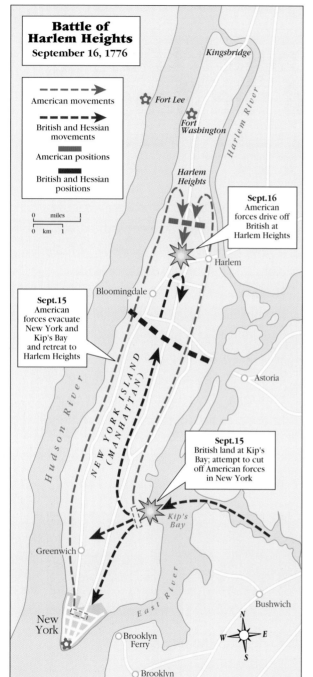

Fort Lee

Fort
Washington

Harlem River

*Harlem
Heights*

Sept.16
American forces drive off British at Harlem Heights

Harlem

Bloomingdale

Sept.15
American forces evacuate New York and Kip's Bay and retreat to Harlem Heights

NEW YORK ISLAND (MANHATTAN)

Hudson River

Astoria

Sept.15
British land at Kip's Bay; attempt to cut off American forces in New York

Kip's
Bay

Greenwich

East River

Bushwich

New
York

Brooklyn
Ferry

N
W   E
S

Brooklyn

across Hollow Way. Music from a British bugler floated through the air. The bugler did not play notes that were used for battle communication, as expected. This bugler played the tune that signaled the end of the chase in a foxhunt, when the hunters have killed the fox. Washington, a foxhunter himself, surely recognized that the Americans were being taunted. His aide, Reed, later described the scene: "The Enemy appeared in open view, & in the most insulting manner sounded their Bugle Horns as is usual after a Fox-Chase. I never felt such a sensation before. It seem'd to crown our Disgrace."

Reed urged Washington to supply reinforcements for the Rangers. Washington did not immediately agree because he feared a repeat of the previous day's humiliation at Kip's Bay. First Washington satisfied himself that large numbers of the enemy were not present across the way. Then he made his plan.

Washington organized a feint from the front. This meant that the Americans would make a false attack to lure the British forward into Hollow Way. Meanwhile, Washington planned to hem the British in. He would send some troops around the British right flank (side) to attack from the rear.

The Battle of Harlem Heights

Around ten o'clock Lieutenant Colonel Archibald Crary of the Rhode Island regiment led the feint with about 150 men from Greene's division. These men entered Hollow Way and posted themselves at the edge of a thick wood. Washington described the scene: "On the appearance of our party in front, they [the British] immediately ran down the Hill, and took possession of some fences and Bushes, and a smart firing began, but at too great a distance to do much execution on either side." Soon, about nine hundred Americans were ordered to support Crary's men. Brisk firing continued for about an hour, still at too far a distance to do much damage. The plan was working. The Americans in front just needed to keep the British busy until the trap could be set.

The Trap Fails

Knowlton and the Rangers were sent to carry out the flanking maneuver. They were joined by Major Andrew Leitch and three companies of riflemen. Leitch and his men came from Virginia, and Washington knew many of them. The goal of the group, about two hundred strong, was to make it to a certain ledge of rocks without being seen.

They did not accomplish their goal. For reasons unknown, the group attacked too soon. Some historians believe that the enemy diverted them somehow, or that some action by the feint group in Hollow Way confused them. Leitch and Knowlton and their troops ended up attacking the flank of the British instead of the rear.

The Rangers and Leitch's men were on a rocky area known as Morningside Heights when their fight with the British flank

The domed library of Columbia University (pictured) sits on the site of the Morningside Heights skirmish.

25

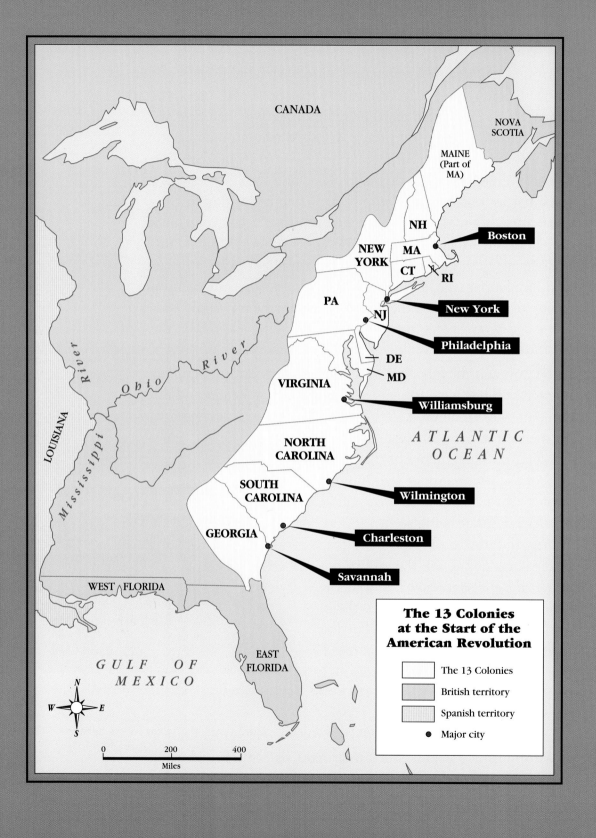

CANADA

NOVA
SCOTIA

MAINE
(Part of
MA)

NH

NEW
YORK

MA

CT

RI

Boston

PA

NJ

New York

Philadelphia

DE

MD

VIRGINIA

Williamsburg

*ATLANTIC
OCEAN*

NORTH
CAROLINA

SOUTH
CAROLINA

Wilmington

GEORGIA

Charleston

Savannah

WEST FLORIDA

Mississippi River

Ohio River

LOUISIANA

*GULF   OF
MEXICO*

EAST
FLORIDA

N
W   E
S

0   200   400
Miles

The 13 Colonies
at the Start of the
American Revolution

The 13 Colonies

British territory

Spanish territory

● Major city

began. A sergeant in the Rangers reported that the British were "posted out of sight on lower ground" and that they opened fire as the Americans reached "the top of the height."

Leitch, in the forefront, received three bullets in his side within minutes. He was quickly carried off the field. Knowlton, fighting near Leitch, was soon hit by a musket ball in his back. Reed put him on his horse and carried him away.

Knowlton died within an hour. Reed reported that the dying Knowlton's only inquiry was "if we had drove the enemy." Another Ranger later described the scene: "My poor Colonel... was shot just by My side.... I took hold of him, asked him if he was badly wounded? He told me he was; but, he says, 'I do not value my Life if we do but get the Day.' ... He desired me by all means to keep up this flank. He seemed as unconcerned and calm as though nothing had happened to him."

Although Washington's plan had not been executed perfectly, the troops' bravery heartened him, and he sent reinforcements. Likewise, the fall of Knowlton and Leitch did not distract the troops from their duties. Meanwhile, at Hollow Way, Greene's and Crary's troops switched from trying to hold the British until the trap could be set, and began a real attack. They forced the enemy to come out from their fence protection. They used artillery to further intimidate the enemy. American general George Clinton reported what happened next: "Our People pursued them closely to the Top of a Hill.... We pursued them to a Buckwheat field on the Top of a high Hill, distance about four hundred paces, where they received a considerable Reinforcement, with several Field Pieces, and there made

American general George Clinton recorded the events of the fight at Hollow Way.

a Stand. A very brisk Action ensued at this place which continued about Two Hours."

The Americans pursued the enemy until, according to Clinton, they "caused them [the British] to fall back into an Orchard, from thence across a Hollow and up another Hill not far distant from their own Lines." Here the Americans abruptly ended the fight. Washington summed it up: "Our troops charged the enemy with great intrepidity, and drove them from the wood into the plain, and were pushing them from thence, having silenced their fire in a great measure, when I judged it prudent to order a retreat." Washington called for the retreat because he believed that British reinforcements were on the way, as indeed they were.

In the early hours of the battle, the British pushed forward about one and one-half miles. By the end, the Americans managed to push the British back the entire distance. The fighting ended at Jones's farmhouse, almost exactly at the same spot where Knowlton's men had first met up with the British at daybreak.

Although British troops marched into New York City on September 19, the American success at Harlem Heights boosted the Continental army's morale.

This engraving depicts the fire that burned much of New York City after the Battle of Harlem Heights. Although they had no proof, the British blamed the Americans.

Numbers of casualties for both sides were hard to pinpoint. It was estimated that the British had about 136 injured and another 35 or more killed, out of approximately 5,000 troops engaged in the battle. American troops involved numbered around 1,800. The American dead numbered around 30, and the missing and wounded numbered slightly less than 100. Leitch was expected to recover from his wounds, but died about two weeks later, as a result of infection.

Epilogue

The Battle of Harlem Heights did not help the Americans gain any ground on New York Island. The battle's importance lies elsewhere—in the morale boost it provided. Washington wrote to Congress, "The affair, I am in hopes will be attended with many salutary [positive] consequences, as it seems to have greatly inspirited the whole of our troops." Reed wrote to his wife, "You can hardly conceive the change it has made in our Army. The men have quite recovered their spirits and feel a confidence which before they had quite lost." The events of September 16 made the Americans realize that if they "stick to these mighty men they [the British] will run as fast as other people," wrote another.

The action at Harlem Heights was typical of Washington's battle plan for much of the war. He knew that his army could rarely beat the British forces in large battles. He thought the best plan was to wear down the enemy with small irritations and annoyances. If the Americans could not win a battle, they at least had to avoid losing.

Sometime during the night of September 20, a fire started in New York City. Soon flames filled the sky. High winds fanned the fire, until it consumed about one-third of the city. Whether the cause was accident or arson has never been determined, but the British blamed the Americans. They rounded up about two hundred suspects during the following weeks as they searched for the perpetrator. No evidence exists that Washington ordered the fire, but he remarked, "Providence [God], or some good honest fellow, has done more for us than we were disposed to do for ourselves."

Washington busied himself immediately after the battle by writing letters to Congress to request more supplies, money, and men for the Continental army. Meanwhile, the British stayed on the plains of Harlem and made no move until October 12. Nevertheless, the Americans lost New York Island before much more time had passed. Washington ordered a retreat from the island on October 16. One month later, the British captured Fort Washington, and after that Fort Lee, just across the Hudson River. Soon thereafter, the British began to chase Washington and the Continental army west across New Jersey.

★

In the summer of 1776 demand for Thomas Paine's pamphlet *Common Sense* grew faster than copies could be printed.

★

The Battle of Harlem Heights

Glossary

adjutant assistant to the commanding officer

aristocrat a person from the upper class

artillery large guns too heavy to carry, such as cannons

battalion a large group of soldiers usually made up of two or more companies

bayonet a detachable blade attached to the muzzle end of a rifle

division military unit

entrenchment a fortification made of trenches

feint a fake attack meant to throw the enemy off guard

flank the extreme left or right side of a group of troops

fortification military defenses such as trenches

Hessian name given to German soldiers employed by the British during the American Revolution

Loyalist colonist who was loyal to the British government; sometimes called Tory

munitions war supplies such as weapons and ammunition

plateau elevated land that is mostly level

regiment military unit that consists of two or more battalions

sovereign the supreme ruler of a country

For More Information

Books

Susan Beller, *American Voices from the Revolutionary War.* Tarrytown, NY: Benchmark Books, 2001.

Janis Herbert, *The American Revolution for Kids: A History with 21 Activities.* Chicago: Chicago Review Press, 2002.

Albert Marrin, *George Washington and the Founding of a Nation.* New York: Dutton Children's Books, 2001.

Stewart Murray, *Eyewitness: American Revolution.* New York: DK, 2002.

Website

Sons of the Revolution in the State of New York
www.sonsoftherevolution.org
Good information about the war in New York.

Index